All the frogs are singing — happiness you're bringing. Hop along! Sing your song!

Swimming, splashing, joking — ribbit, ribbit, croaking. "Come along! Join the song!"

English text copyright © 2012 by North-South Books Inc., New York 10017.
Original Title: Chœur de grenouilles
© 2011 Mijade Publications (B-Namur–Belgium)
© 2011 Annick Masson for the illustrations
© 2011 Luc Foccroulle for the text

First published in the United States, Great Britain, Canada, Australia, and
New Zealand in 2012 by North-South Books, Inc., an imprint of NordSüd
Verlag AG, CH-8005 Zürich, Switzerland.

Translated by Sabina Touchburn.
Designed by Pamela Darcy.
Distributed in the United States by North-South Books Inc., New York 10017.
Library of Congress Cataloging-in-Publication Data is available.
ISBN: 978-0-7358-4062-1 (trade edition)
1 3 5 7 9 • 10 8 6 4 2
Printed in Belgium by Proost N.V., B 2300 Turnhout, November 2011.
www.northsouth.com

Bertha and the Frog Choir

By Luc Foccroulle   Illustrated by Annick Masson

NorthSouth
New York / London

It's not easy being a frog!
The other animals are so beautiful.

The fox has such silky fur. . . .

The swan has such majestic feathers. . . .

The butterfly's wings are so shimmery. . . .

But frogs . . . they are quite flabby and slimy.

Yuck!

What we DO like about frogs . . . is their chorus!

And what every frog dreams about is one day being part of the choir.

Today was Bertha's BIG day. Her parents were
so proud of her.

Her father said in a serious tone, "My dear Bertha,
you are grown up now. It's time to show the world
what you're capable of doing!"

Bertha got in line behind her friend.
"Oh, my goodness! What a crowd," she said.

"Hi, Lucy! What's wrong? You're trembling like a leaf!"
"I'm terrified!" said Lucy. "I've been preparing for this
moment for such a long time."

"Don't worry!" said Bertha.
"You're talented. You're sure to
make a good impression!
    "I, on the other hand . . ."
    "Next!" cried Amadeus, the choir leader.

The candidates filed past. It was a croaking and singing festival as the frogs practiced their lines:

"Let it be, let it be, let it be, let it beeeee. . . ."

"We are the frogs, we are the children. . . ."
"We are the frogs who make a brighter day. . . ."

"I will surviiive! YEAH! YEAH!"

At last it was Lucy's turn. But before she could sing a single note,
Amadeus shouted:

"What are you doing here? You're much too little for our choir!"

"But . . . but . . . just let me sing something . . . ," cried Lucy.

"TUT! TUT! TUT! NEXT!" said the choir leader.

Bertha was next.

"Ah, finally someone who's the right size!"
cried Amadeus.

"Show us what you can do!"

ALL MY FRAWGS...croak!

Bertha began to sing, and the strangest,
most shocking sounds came out of her mouth!
"Enough!! That's TERRIBLE!" shouted the choir leader.
"What a disgrace to our species! NEXT!"

Bertha's heart sank. She joined Lucy on the edge of the pond. They were both so unhappy.

"You're not alone," said Bertha. "It looks like we both failed! You're too small, and I can't sing to save my life.

"But I have an idea! When I'm sad, I make myself a nice meal.

"I'm going to cook up a delicious soup. It will help you grow, and you can teach me how to sing. OKAY?"

Lucy agreed. She slurped up
Bertha's slug soup, fly broth, lily
pad stew, . . . and little by little
Lucy's courage returned.

Now it was time for Bertha's singing lessons.
Bertha, gave it her all. . . .

Unfortunately, without any success!
"I think it's hopeless!" said Bertha.
"I sing just as badly as before, and
you're still just as small. . . ."

"Hmmmm! I have an idea,"
said Lucy. "Come over here and open
your mouth as wide as you can!"

HOP!
Little Lucy jumped right into Bertha's mouth.
"W'at 'R' yOU dOIN'?"

"Hush! Be quiet and listen," said Lucy.
Then she began to sing a beautiful melody
with all her heart:

"One day . . . my prince will come. . ."

"I UN'ERstan'. y'UR I'EA's GREAt!"
"Let's go get 'em! We're going to impress
everyone," whispered Lucy.

The next day, Bertha auditioned for a second time in front of Amadeus. Everyone was completely charmed!

"It's wonderful! It's marvelous! You have made incredible progress. Congratulations, Bertha. You deserve a place as a soloist for the prince's wedding!"

Their trick worked like a charm,
aside from Lucy becoming quite
wet and slimy.

Bertha felt guilty when her parents congratulated
her. But putting that aside, she and Lucy were quite
happy, and no one had found out their hoax!

It was the prince's wedding day. . . .
All the frogs were clearing their throats backstage.

Lucy was surprised not to see Bertha.
She looked everywhere, and finally
found her . . . in the kitchen.

The chefs were surrounding Bertha,
congratulating her for the delicious
fly-and-slug terrine she had prepared.

"But . . . what are you doing? You aren't ready?"

"I'VE HAD ENOUGH!" said Bertha. "Everyone admires YOUR beautiful voice! As soon as you're big enough, you won't need me anymore. What am I supposed to do?"

"But we agreed."
"No, it was your idea!
I just want to be a CHEF!"

Lucy hadn't thought of it in that way.

"You're right!" said Lucy. "We'll tell them that we deserve more than half an invitation to this wedding!"

"That won't be necessary. . . . I heard everything!" exclaimed Amadeus. "I thought something fishy was going on, and it's time we did something about it!"

"Lucy, despite your small size,
you have proven that you deserve
a place in our choir.

"As for you, Bertha . . . you have
a real talent for cooking, and we'll
be needing your help today!"

As far as beautiful weddings go . . .
the prince's wedding was a real beauty.

"I told you," said Lucy. "All's well that ends well. Thanks to me!"

"You must be joking? I was the one who dared!"

"Well, no, it was me!"

"No, it was me!"

"It was me!"

"No, me!"

Sing to the tune of "Frère Jacques"